SISTERHOOD

SISTERHOOD

CODY ADAM

CONTENTS

Sisterhood
By Cody Adam

Contents

Beginnings

Sunday April 6, 1997
High School Graduation Year
"We are one before you, Great spirit" all four friends in bond said.

"I'm North" Sara whitewater said while holding a razor.

"I'm east," Vicky Jackson said while holding a sharpened pocket-knife.

"I'm south," Grace Smith said while holding a razor too.

"I'm west," Courtney Becks said while holding a kitchen steak knife.

"Together we are the sisterhood," Grace said

"Together we are the sisterhood," Vicky said

"Together we are the sisterhood," Sara said

"Together we are the sisterhood," Courtney said

They cut their right palm, slice open blood pouring into a silver cup having a cross at the bottom on four sides of the cup. "Our blood is companion to you, great spirit", Grace said. "It connects to our flesh," Vicky said, "Flesh then connects to our soul," Sara said, "Soul then connects to spirit," Courtney said. "Consume the gateway to our existence great spirit." All four said as once, there are twelve candles lit in a circle, the four friends in sisterhood in the circle close together with salt also making the circle, and the windows of the cabin are open for the natural air at this location. "Now we put our scared elements that will connect to the great spirit in the cup of our sisterhood." Grace said. "I put earth," Sara said while pouring a handful of soil into the silver cup having their four-blood mixed in. "I put flight animal: a bird feather," said Vicky putting a feather of an eagle in the cup. "I put man," Courtney said putting a handful of a male's regional hair in the cup. "I put plants," Grace said putting a regular plant as you would see in a park in the cup with its roots. Grace then gets a rock form tool for crushing things like pills or roots and crushes the items with the blood in the cup passing it along to her now sisters for them to crush by having their energy with their blood mixed together gives the power of connect in their sisterhood by all four doing the act of mixing their elements to their great spirit inside an empty thick wooden floor room at Grace Smith's relative's cabin near a lake in Oklahoma. "Makes us supreme nature to be done, our existence is yours to keep," Grace begins. "In the arms of you great spirit in glorifying scenes, we are yours to keep," Vicky said continuing. "May we never be in sin to weep, for great spirit we are yours to keep," Sara said also continuing. "To the end of this realm be with us for the next stage of life for we offer this sisterhood for you great spirit to keep, Amen" Courtney ended the chant. Suddenly the twelve candles fire blew out, and then the candles fire again more brightly and more scent from the candles in the room. "Yes, the glimpse, the fresh air will be nicer to us without sickness," Grace said pointing out what just happened from the fire and the candle manner. "Flash with the candles, supernatural. Knew it all along." Sara said still standing along with her other sisters in the circle. "It's done for sure; our lifelong pack confirm by the nature of fire lighting a candle in its way of naturally becoming witch." Courtney said. "The pack of supernatural to the regular eyes, it's our great spirit we owe to in life for our fire to be witch has ignited." Vicky said as she walks out of the circle. The sisters then leave the candles lit on the floor and the cup with the blood and their elements connecting to their great spirit mixed together is sealed now in the middle as they break the circle looking upon the candles. Grace looks upon the cup in the middle with pleasure knowing all what's in the cup is for spells to do for the common good of their sisterhood lives. The rest of the sisters are in awe too of what they have done and what's instore for their supernatural future from the book that taught them how to be.

Saturday, October 13, 1888
New York City, New York

"Push!" "Breathe!" "Push!" Crying sound comes to hear, a fresh female baby being born. "Good! Now her twin." The doctor said readying to guide the birth. The mother looks upon the father in sweat with great awe in giving birth, realizing it's almost done. "Push!" "Breathe!" "Last Push!" Baby's feet showing first. The doctor force his hands in the vagina, grabs the baby out and unties the womb's cord from the baby's neck wrapped halfway. "No!" The father cried. "Hurry, check the baby," the doctor said leading the baby towards the nurse. The nurse grabs the baby, does her routine checking the baby to see if the baby has life, and confirms the baby is dead. "What's wrong Clyde?" The mother asks the father in relief of pressure as she is seeing the nurse talking to the doctor and her husband while holding the baby. "One of our daughters did not make it, my Isabella." The father tells his wife the mother of the twins in tears mixed emotions for happy to have given birth and having depressed tears for seeing one of his daughters dead at birth. "No, Cly!" the mother cries. The father brings the dead child to the mother. The mother holds her dead child in her arms, staring with tears of hurt coming down her cheek and she then determines her demeanor towards Godly thoughts. "You just needed to go to heaven early my beloved, Norma." The mother said rubbing her hand on the baby's cheeks and head while the father nods on, agreeing. "Father has plans for you and Mary this way, we will see you when we arrive in time Norma, happy birthday, Baby!" The mother continues assuring herself and her dead child while the father weeps in agreement. Mary the alive twin gets carries to the father after the nurse cleanse her, "Tell your sister goodbye Mary." The father brings the child to her dead twin in the mother's arms. The father kneels and prays while the mother tears herself in awe and sorrow handling it well looking at her husband praying by the bedside.

Monday, October 13, 1958
New York City, New York

"This book will be our element after I die, leaving a power on earth to form into goodness, my Norma. My life works in not living a life just being with you as you showed me your presence from the other side to keep me at bay, grant us this witchcraft book to be real as we are real connecting to each other as one is deceased since birth." Mary said using a typewriter and having drawing pencils near for any illustrations need to be done for this book she is making with her twin sister being the reason of supernatural phenomenon in her life and liking more to do with the supernatural in her life to make her twin powerful with her aging to be dead in the near decades to have her be ready to be accepted on the other side which she call the boundary of heaven upon the earth. Suddenly she takes the paper out of the typewriter and unlocks the typewriter to get the ink cartridge. She opens the ink lightly and quickly grabs a pocketknife from her kitchen countertop middle drawer. She cuts her index finger and drips the blood into the ink and a lot of it to soak with the ink. She attends to the cut by putting a bandage around her finger. Loads the ink cartridge with her blood into the typewriter, puts a new paper in the roll, and begins typing, "First love in bound," she types. "The blood is our imprint on this earth from and of our connection to the creator, my sister Norma," she whispers and then continues to type. "First step of this holiness way is for two elements separate or together. Something or Someone, have it in mind, something has a true meaning, and someone has a true life. Your first sight on that something or someone has life; you recognize it, or someone is alive. Then you are born into this world, living and breathing come to know this something or someone you are connected to has no life no more; it or someone is dead never going to be in your flesh living with its flesh meaning next to you or have life with you throughout your life, so you come to an agreement; a pact to not live a life which comes survival and wisdom in life. Meaning don't have a husband or a wife for the someone, and don't use another thing that is the same thing for the something as in not using a structure no more for is died out. There are other ways as well but that's the main vow, never marry and have children for the someone, and never use identical thing as the something. Master that and patience with your vow has the great spirit being loved with you, the great spirit will allow natural events happen in your life for your wellbeing and the common good." She pauses typing, "You are my great spirit, my sister. God allowed you to come in spirit to me giving your flesh look alike me in vision states by my vow, God allowing, you are the great spirit my Norma, best sister in the world as I love you dearly with my blood being the energy to spark this witchcraft to happen, it will make you more powerful in the father's existence for our wellbeing of everlasting life and the common good," Mary said smiling knowing her proof of God comes from her vow she made since she was able to think on her own is to not live a life for her twin sister died at birth and not living a life with her, or so she thought.

On her 17 birthday she saw her twin sister in spiritual formation as in flesh naked upon her grave as Mary was there on their birthday celebrating the last years of being a child, the weather was in mid-sixties degrees with the fall breeze being kind to you. She was shocked at first then all was calm for her faith in God courage her to take the supernatural event in a normal state, "It's you Norma, same red hair as me and naked!" She said to her after realizing a person looking like her appearing out of nowhere near her tombstone. "Yes, here to watch you celebrate us being close to adults now, your love has guided me to father it's the light in the darkness which is good and has father with you as I'm with you for you are goodness" Norma said to her as she sat down next to her flesh soul, and spirit living twin: Mary. "I have so many questions, my sister!" "Only God our father has the answers, silly!" Norma replied realizing her sister was in awe. "Let's just enjoy this moment as it last forever, my sister." Norma said to her as Mary smiles took out her hand and gave it to her sister, and Norma held it. Mary felt her spiritual formation sister's hand in fleshy cooling grip.

She goes back in typing, "As said with patience in doing this type of love action creates a bond with the great spirit and return the great spirit may reward you in the favor of the great spirit upon you in life together with the great spirit. Have faith, be determined in doing that love act, don't live a life for that someone or something. Just survive until your end of this world while you don't live a life for this loved one or loving thing is the focus of this love in bond of the great spirit. The energy made by devoting your life in not having a life or not getting the something in natural need for today's world is a light shown to someone or something on the other side which is heaven. The someone could be a mother, father, close friend, sister, brother and the something would be the necessity of the great spirit like a chariot, holy bible, temple, cross, plants and trees or stones. A definition in that nature is life and meaning of someone or something being your chosen element with the great spirit." She pauses for a moment to drink her cup of her own made tea with saying a prayer beforehand, "Dear lord, I ask the weather still be stable here until I go to my twin sister in your kingdom, may the weather be stable for human anywhere my book is made in Jesus Christ, amen." She whispers this prayer again and drinks her tea in calming mood with joy remembering her twin that day for their imprint of the supernatural that is natural to her to live. She goes back to typing, "This energy made from the vow living will be the connection to the energy to do for the common good, which is the wisdom brought to you with your someone or something on the other side. Not living a life for a dead temple will greet the temple of the great spirit as for the same in not living a life for a father will greet the father of the great spirit. As doing so will have a meet with the someone or something in time for the light made will attract them to you. This energy made will have ability to do the common good for you in this living world as we know it. Weather is one, you will always be in good weather rather the rain or snow is needed it will come when its truly needed. You may notice the weather is worst at other parts of the world, you then thank the great spirit and pray for their weather be stable for the energy of connecting to the someone or something on the other side has it strengthen ability to do so with having natural faith as well." She pauses and looks at the lettering on the paper and notices her energy from her blood is being imprinted well with the ink being the direction of this book to leave a legacy with her twin on earth. She gets up and walks to her kitchen, washes her hands with her own made soap. And she walks back to her table in the dining room of her house she made into an art studio for her book, picks up a pencil and draws on the paper. She makes a dot for each of the four directions, makes a smaller dot for the four corners of the directions with two dots for each corner. She then labels each dot with length measurement candles having the four directions candles bigger than the four corner directions. She makes four patterns of these stating the point is from the south to go clock wise, point from the north to go clock wise, point from the west to go clock wise, point from the east to go clock wise for stepping in the circle made of candles, lighting the candles from the point, blowing out the candles from the point, and making energy ability in the circle standing at the point. She labels all four to give the stage see in what to do for the boundary opening from the other side which is heaven. She then stops stares at what she did and agrees she is doing it right, she walks to her typewriter sits down to begin typing from where she left off, and suddenly she passes out, collapses on the chair to the ground. The eyes of Mary open but the sight of life is from her twin Norma. "Let's see what I can put down for you." Norma giggles as she takes over her twin's body. "I know you are making a book to be powerful with our lives twine in it." She sits on the chair begins typing, "A circle making with four humans together for the common good." She stops typing and speaks, "Let's make it for a sisterhood with us being the powerful connect to father, I see the great spirit is what you call me and father, very well, my Mary." She continues the sentence, "with the great spirit interacting having a pleasure with the beings the great spirit has created, with your touch my sister the way of bond only for someone and living something like a plant or soil the earth in the goal for the common good. With your faith in me sister we will be powerful to uphold a circle of four for the common good of life until the return of the king Jesus Christ. Form a structure the ways of getting the power to do so from our father the great spirit, as your bond with him in loving me the way you do, remember the weather, it's always right with you wherever you go you will always receive nice weather, for our energy gives positive feedback to the natural world. Start this book new starting for four females of age into sisterhood that forms a love connection to the element that is a symbol to the great spirit, and we will take care of the selected after you come here with me as I show up in the supernatural way from our great spirit-Norma. She then gets up, walks to Mary's couch which is a few feet away in the living room and lays down to go to sleep.

Mary wakes up, refreshed attends to the bathroom relieve herself while noticing the felt of peeing was more tender than before with satisfaction of releasing the urine. She goes to her office area for her teacup and grabs it, "whoa, more lines?" She asks out loud, noticing a few extra sentences on the manuscript of her ideal book and reads it then says, "A book design for four as one circle of sisterhood from our power, my sister Norma, so be it." She completes the book later in the year.

Friday, March 23, 2007
Ten years later
"All of what I'm doing will regain your vision back, okay?" Courtney Becks said to 33-year age women in the four-sisterhood's garage attached to their home having the garage door open to enjoy the perfect spring weather with its breeze being an element of this spell to do. Courtney then draws a cross and a circle with her dead grandmother's ashes on this 33-year age women's forehead as she is laying down on a massage table having no glasses on her vision is very blurry with spots. Courtney then squeezes a half slice orange above this women's right eye having it juice enter her right eye and Courtney does do with the other eye. "Aww, it burns" the women said. She then rubs the juice in her eyes by her hands, "Man to

see the father in Jesus Christ's name, amen" Courtney prays as she done wiping the juice in the women's eyes with her having a little scream from the burning. Courtney then wipes her eyes with a wet towel wet by natural faucet water. "Sorry for the burn, orange has its ability to help our immune system," Courtney said. As this woman wipes her eyes, she notices her sight is normal, "Whoa, it worked and I did not believe you, Courtney! I can see and the spots are not there! Thank you very much! The 33-year-old women said wiping her eyes in joy. "You are very welcome, miss Sheila there is a God and we will be judge for our life." Courtney replies, leading her out of the garage. "Yes, there is a God by orange juice I can see, awesome!" Sheila says as she leaves waving goodbye to Courtney. Courtney then closes the garage door and goes into the house.

"Sara! Grace! Your orange from the tree youse planted work fabulous! Courtney said going into the kitchen as all three sisters are there as well at the wooden circle table having the cup they use for the ceremony forming their sisterhood gaining the great spirit ability in their lives, the one cup that ties their blood with their element connection to the great spirit; the symbol of their birth of becoming witches at the center of the table. "You should know by now all wonders will work with the great spirit being our master," Sara said sipping on her own made tea. "Yeah, but it's always shocking to me to see such wonders being lively." Courtney said and she sits down at the table joining her sisters. "Blessed roots of the tree in the blessed soil of earth will do the blessings, glad it worked, Courtney!" Grace said, who is also sipping on tea that Sara made. "Another good thing we did, another day as we." Vicky said who is sipping on red wine. The aftermath winter breeze blowing through the windows with the land once again meeting the heatwaves of the sun in the spring thrills the women in joy of satisfaction having their senses heighten over the years praying to the great spirit and having a bond with their connection to the great spirit with receiving blessings to dwell with in their element connection with the great spirit. "The weather is made of paradise and today's weather is the continue of it." Sara said, enjoying her homemade tea. "What's next on the agenda?" Vicky asks the ladies enjoying the breeze coming in the kitchen windows. "Going to the park sometime to pray for no sin be lively in man in the open wind." Courtney said while sipping on the tea Sara had made. The three drinking the tea Sara made are really relaxed in their seat now. "I mean anybody we can heal again or actual do some action?" Vicky said, getting a buzz from her red wine. "The animal needs to let loose?" Grace asks Vicky. Vicky giggles, "Naw, just like to do some action where it benefits the goodness of our ability to life with the great spirit." Vicky replies having no intention to do nothing. "Yes, let's make a huge impact in loving the great spirit in doing something, since then was minor acts in what we been doing," Courtney said having a direction to do while continuing drinking Sara's homemade tea. "Evolution growth with the great spirit, have our energy spark it in births in a prayer ceremonial." Sara adds while looking at the two drinking her homemade tea recognizing they are influenced by the tea. "Yes, have a circle energy form in this city and have it touch births for here on out for life with the great spirit is everlasting." Vicky describes more of the idea of what to do while feeling the loose buzz from the red wine that she is drinking. "I love that the idea, it's a spark of life away from sin and faith with the great spirit of our bond together being the energy to make it happen, let's do it." Grace says still being relaxed from the effects of the tea. "I will look at the book that formed us to find a way." Courtney says with excitement pouring her another cup of Sara's homemade tea. "Your tea from the blessed soil it grew from is very good, Sara" Courtney says enjoying the taste of the tea and how smooth it goes down the throat. "Thanks, it is mixed with other plants; it's for relaxing and immune health with touch of hallucination if you drink a lot for the stomach to absorb." Sara replies. Courtney then gets up out of the chair, "I'm going to head into the book and find us a way." Courtney says and leaves the kitchen area. "I got a copy of the book I'm go to help find a way too." Sara says and leaves the kitchen. Grace then asks, "Lend me her hand and close your eyes." Vicky does so, "Mirror to the eye, die the hair red for the blood of our guy the great spirit, amen" Grace said in a chanting sound, "Now open your eyes," Vicky opens her eyes realizing Grace blonde hair is not blonde no more its red. "Your hair is red, Grace!" "Yes, I like it, anything symbolizing the great spirit we can fashion." Grace replies. "Well, I've been working on flight, with a straight pole or a stick, holding it vertical lifts you, then point it straight levels you, point it diagonally you go forward but in going up, point is down you go down as you able to ride it. I can feel the pole or the stick if its steel or wood I can feel its lifeform helping me to begin flight but need to be used for the common good of things, can't waste that ability." Vicky said smiling while having a drink of her red wine. "That's good, I'm sure in need might be handy to know the power of flight, but with your height there is no need to fly," Grace giggles. "No kidding, shorty! It's fantastic that the great spirit can let me possess the power of flight, yet I know the bond we have is for the common good, to flight without proper meaning might be no good, unless it's really a need I will do it." Vicky says detailing her consciousness about the ability she has from the bond she made with the animal bird with the great spirit in always having food for the wild birds that surrounds their home in Broken Arrow , Oklahoma in thought to give life to other birds in joy from missing her only pet, it was a bird as birds are sociable creatures she believes her bird would enjoy the company of feeding other birds as being the alpha of the flock. Grace and Vicky conversate for hours from day into the night about the means of common good and thoughts to go with their next move drinking on their drinks that has effects of satisfaction feeling while Sara and Courtney do their homework on their mission to have a huge impact in life.

Sunday, March 25, 2007

"As this Sunday we worship the great spirit as usual with our steps on the next mission of our list of spells, Courtney and I did our research." Sara said as she is standing in the living room next to the coffee table in front of the couch where the sisters are sitting enjoying their nectar drink mix with moonshine in top of the afternoon as they prayed to their great spirit and talked about the word of God on how he doesn't give up on his creation having Jesus Christ saved the world of humans as the message is the inspiring feeling for them to do their next mission in forming a spell to advance humanity out of the darkness. "First of all this spell is to enhance the birth of humanity away from sin, by their natural habit will be against sin and having the chemicals in their brain being formed to enjoy life without sin, this having a possible major change in history depending how mature in wise with the energy to do so since sin is everywhere in this country." Sara explains being excited. "Courtney connection is man, which we need her period blood, it symbol is birth. Vicky connection is the bird, we need an egg, its symbol is energy for man and birthing. Grace connection is plants, we need roots of plants only for its symbol is health for man in growth from birth. And I am earth which we need is soil which symbolizes the habitat of man the home of life for man. All mixed together then salt poured on them, we say our prayer and the items will ignite, be on fire until it burns out. Then we will know it worked that way, and we do this every year since then with our proof of the great spirit the spell will be intact in working progress until its complete, as we can find out someway the effect of the spell is working by getting the generation statistics from schools and within that type of identifying the generations, as well finding out the births if they were successful and finding out how many were not and keep track of that every year , Courtney suggested which is great homework, but our faith in the great spirit and his love for us will make this major impact happen." Sara finished explaining and sits on the loveseat turns on the music which is nature sounds from their stereo hook up in the living room. "The elements will muster the energy for our spell to work for it is the symbol of our connection to the great spirit, glory to the great spirit," Grace said then takes a drink of their homemade influenced liquid. "To have a section of humanity be against sin and have the will to do something about it like our immune system, it's against all negative invaders and in growth has the will to block sickness from happening." Courtney adds on while taking a drink as well. "Be able to trust strangers and the strangers be able to trust you for sin is not in their habitat nature." Vicky said too, about the effects of their spell having the means of a huge impact of life. "Glory to the great spirit our creator of means to live." Grace praises as she raises her drink in toast then takes a drink. "Amen," the three sisters said after Grace.

The impact

Sunday, April 15, 2007
Broken Arrow, Oklahoma

"This evening, great spirit is the start of our mission, a spell that will have none depart from you." Sara said lighting up the twelve candles with a match around a tree stump in their backyard starting from the northeast point for its where the sisterhood is located on the earth and lighting the candles clockwise from the northeast point. "Births," Sara said putting soil on the tree stump. "Generations," Grace said putting plant roots on the tree stump. "Living," Vicky said putting a wild bird egg on the tree stump too. "Creator," Courtney said putting a paper towel soaked with her blood from her period cycle upon the tree stump as well. Then they all pour a half palm size filled with salt on the objects on the tree stump. The four sisters notice the natural breeze is picking up as they stand north, east, south, and west holding their hands together and breathing at the same time as the candles are lit around them with the tree stump in the middle of them. "Great spirit! Forth the energy to comprehend no sin," Sara said in chanting while lifting up her hands connected to her sisters. "Great spirit! Forth the energy of bravery to end the life of sin," Vicky continues the chant lifting up her hands as well. "Great spirit! Forth the energy in natural dwelling of no sin," Grace continues the chant as she lifts up her hands too. "Great spirit forth the energy with everlasting promise of hatred towards sin," Courtney said ending the prayer as she lifts up her hands and the four sisters has their hands up in the air while their hands interlocking with each other's, "Amen!" All four sisters said swinging their hands down as they their hands came to their waist the candles blew out from the breeze that was getting little windier, then dead silence appears having no wind as the sisters still breathing at the same time, they look at the center tree stump they kneel down next to it still in a circle, "Forth the energy!" They all said at the same time. Suddenly the candles are lit again with a bigger flame and the salt on the objects on the tree stump begins a flame, burning the objects, and lighting the backyard as the sun disappears in the night. All four sisters get up from kneeling apart their hands holding from clockwise direction departing from the north and so forth and they stare at the top of the flaming tree stump while smelling the candles more brightly in their backyard. "It's the start, now we keep doing this every year and keep the faith to make the strength of this spell work over the years." Sara said to her sister smiling having proof from the candles and the fire that its bound. "Yes, the time to gather the elements has it's worth, now naturally humanity will not easily sin as we do this every year and makes ways of faith to strengthen this spell as time passes." Courtney said being excited for the future. "Praise the great spirit for our work will be complete," Grace said being amused as they continue to stare at the tree stump firing on top, looking at the burning soil and the cooking egg while the paper towel soaked in blood slowly burns with the roots having the strongest odor in the flame. "May we be together as always for our hearts is with the common good and the light is good, we make the light in the darkness of times in during the return of the king, praise the great spirit, amen." Vicky adding her sense in having her passion to be a witch being satisfied now.

As all sisters agreeing on the fire being the sign that the spell is bound, Vicky's late pet parrot suddenly lands on her right shoulder as the sisters were staring at the fire on the tree stump. "Jupiter! It's you!" Vicky quickly pets her dead yet alive pet parrot on its red feathered head and he speaks," Aak Vicky, Good, Aak," while standing on her shoulder then he lifts up gets two wing flaps then disappears in thin air. The other three sisters are in more awe seeing Vicky's bird showing up as the objects and the candles are burning after being lit up by the energy of their Great Spirit by their power to spell. The three sisters then close their eyes and begin to pray, noticing Vicky dead pet bird came alive after the spell showing himself to her is a good omen. They open their eyes, done praying and they are seeing a smile on Vicky.

September 25, 1990

Village for the Seniors – Albany, New York

102-year aged Mary finishes drinking her hot honey tea in her bedroom, turns off the television which was on CNN broadcast, and she gently moves in the bed under the puffed cotton cover blanket to go to sleep. Thirty minutes goes by and she is deep asleep, "Mary almost time," Mary sees her twin sister as young as 17 years of age in their childhood home recognizing it's a dream state vision. "Norma! This dream is at home. They tore down this house in the 1930s." "Yes, a dream, but you are not going to wake up again sister to the living. We both came into this world together and we shall leave this world together, your devoted love shined the light to have me come to you which father saw it was good, now we are young again to leave and go rest together with the energy we leave on earth in the living father in our dimension ways of connecting with each other like now in reality from the other side will glory the good we have lived in our path sister, Our energy the book we made will be good to the world until the next age of humanity who are also good at the end of this age, it's time! Ma and Pa had made it there waiting." Mary stares at her twin sister realizing the years they had hasn't had an awe until this point of her natural life and gives her hand to Norma both wearing matching white dresses that matches the light beyond the door showing through the windows in the door having curtains in the corners of the thick wooden door windows beaming with light on the other side. "Let's go," Norma said as she opens the door taking a step into the light with her twin sister following her, who never quite lived a life, yet her dream career life was to be a lawyer and get involved with politics and have a seat somewhere in a house of government, but she just collected money from her heir of tea and coffee company her parents owned as her grandparents on her mother side owned and she has not been married or had a boy-friend to experience romance as in first kiss nor losing her virginity. They both feel the bright light in their existence, feeling calm, more aware of who they are, so as to gently swift away in the air and they simply go to rest.

Mary was found by the village nurse; the village health center Identify the death in heart failure: her beating heart slowed until it stopped making it natural death due to her age.

Thursday, March 9, 2017

Broken Arrow, Oklahoma

Twenty Years Later

"It's our tenth anniversary of the impactful spell that leads to have harden faith, next month we will bring the energy ten years strong. Any news about our spell since we were quiet about it even though we do the spell every year, but does anyone have results to say?" Sara asks her sisters as they are gathered in the kitchen of their finally paid off home at the circular table that comes out bigger once you rotate it clockwise.

"In matter of fact, I have been keeping tabs on certain things, like locally this city alone has one disabled baby out of 2,000 births, about 2,223 births a year here, starting from 2008 to now. In the teen age years going to adult, locally the graduation percentage is up high only one student doesn't graduate a year since 2008 by now all students graduate, all local," Courtney replies being comfortable sitting on a wooden chair with a pillow seat. " The wild of birds been producing more in Tulsa here in this state." Vicky mentions sipping on her home made wine, she made it with Grace, but only made for her for the other three sisters enjoy hallucination drinks, mostly marijuana mix with the herbs that has potential to get you high, with the marijuana for sure going to get you high in being mix with others with the potential they really depend on it mostly for worshipping the great spirit saying the great spirit is high stable all the time and more stable high happy when we come forth to him, they decided about the plants that able to get you feeling better as being stone is what the Great Spirit mood is all the time like unlocking a secret about the creator's actual being existence being.

"The might of the bird gets its food regardless, our faith will be reality one day, regardless." Vicky also mentions having high hopes for their craft being strong. "So far plants are stable to supply countries, going to take faith for them to complete healing factors for the serious illness, which I have knowingly it takes a right lifestyle for all to produce rightfully starting at birth, same with the plants starting at their birth we can trigger evolution for man, that's my faith. Also, it's working by the negative in the world, mass shootings are happening on the regular which the power force attacks the bad, the bad will best to conquer it," Grace says having feedback of what the spell is. "Well, my report is our faith sisters, as well do this for the tenth year, we will complete the faith to have it reality living among us in strength. As well bumping into an angry person and the person says sorry or you say sorry and nothing bad happen we forgives and move on." Sara speaks her value towards the spell they are doing, all sitting around the table drinking the liquids that influence your mood.

Friday, March 10, 2017

"Lively roots, be the one," Grace digs in the dirt with her hand shovel around a wild plant exposing the roots. She digs until she is able to grab the roots with ease. Her right hand is around the healthy roots, she pulls where there is enough length to have it break. It breaks, suddenly the roots transform into a snake dinosaur type creature in her hand getting bigger where she drops it on the ground. She stands up moves a feet away, and the transformation is done for the creature the snake dinosaur like creature slithers around then raises its head to her level being about six foot in length where Grace stands five foot and four inches, "Flower child, what have you done?" the snake dinosaur like creatures asks her. Grace pauses in fright realizing this is happening at a park in the city with no one around at the moment and it can talk then she gets calm realizing experiencing the supernatural is normal "Done nothing wrong, What are you?" She asks the creature with its tongue smelling around. " Surly you know about the beast in the garden, flower child and know the blood of father is tasty. Realize what you have done! Are you wise enough to unspell your doing?" "What are you talking about unspell, my doing? ... Garden. The beast. Oh!", Grace recognizes the creature happens to be the serpent. "Did the great spirit punish you for interrupting the head of man?" Grace asks in bravery. "Flower child, it's my nature to make sin happen to the creation of man, unspell your doing for it tempers, dandy my anger!" The serpent then slithers fast around Grace in a circle and stops in front of her raises up then dissolves into the healthy roots she picked for the tenth anniversary ceremony of the spell to enhance man to not sin. She picks them up, looking at them, "You're the one." Grace says without hesitation and knows now these roots are the one. She walks on , heading home.

While Grace is walking home Sara twists the knob towards off and there is a line of water trailing out of the faucet still. She then looks under the sink to find anything unusual that might need a simple fix. She looks for minutes not seeing any problems, and gets back up standing and seeing the thin streak of water pouring into the sink. She turns the knob to on, thick water pours out of the faucet, and then she turns it off hoping it will be off this time. Nope, the water pours out in a think streak line into the sink. Suddenly the thin line water transforms into the serpent in the sink, filling the sink. "What in the name of Jesus!" "Earth child, the name of Jesus would not dwell, undo your annoying spell!" Sara taking the sight in of a creature being form from water with ability to talk and tells her to undo what they're doing. She remains calm, "You want me to undo my spell, come into existence just to have me undo a spell, which means you are an enemy. Be out of sight and bound by the judgement of the great spirit!" a loud hiss sounds the kitchen from the serpent. "You will see and then realize you are no match for the mighty best in the garden, earth child." The serpent said as it is moving back n forth in the sink then sticks it head into the faucet quickly transforms back to thin streaking water out of the faucet. Sara angrily twists the knob on and quickly off with this time the water stays off.

Grace makes it home, goes to the backdoor of the house where it's connected to the kitchen and Sara is there at the table praying. Grace tosses the healthy roots on the table, "Never guess what I have experience?" Grace says as she heads to pour her some home-made tea made mixed with ingredients like the psych medication Trazadone. "I bet I can. Have you met an enemy of a snake like that can talk?" Sara asks. "Yeah, the serpent!" Grace confirms. "Told you to undo a spell?" Sara asks. "Yeah, unspell a spell for it makes him angry." "Yeah, me too it transforms from water in our house." Sara mentions. "It came from the these roots I pick for our prayer cere-mony which is the spell it is referring, I believe." Grace also mentions quickly sipping on her tea. Then she sits down next to Sara," We have to alert the others." Grace says, "Yes, form a protection spell, too!" Sara gets up and calls the other sisters to come into the kitchen.

"What it is darling?" Vicky asks as she enters the kitchen with Courtney passing her to seat herself at the table. "Grace and I have exciting news but brace yourself." Vicky seats herself at the table with the others. "Sara and I met the serpent alone today me while getting the wild roots at the nearby park, the color is green thick scales as it skin with it form like a ancient snake and was able to talk to me and to Sara, wanting us to undo the spell we have been doing." "You mean the serpent from the Bible appeared to you both!?" Vicky asks, "Yes!" Sara answers. "The enemy of man, means we are on the right track and got to be prepared for anything, sisters!" Courtney says with little worry. "Well, we need to do a protection spell soon." Sara suggests, "Yes I agree have the holy Bible involved for me my side of the circle," Courtney said being less worrisome. Grace sipping on her influenced tea and Sara grabs Grace and Courtney's hand as Vicky sees she grabs their hand as well making a circle, "Dear Great Spirit find a way for light to overcome the darkness in our circle of sisterhood, Amen." Sara prayed, "Amen!" the three sisters said agreeing to the prayer.

During that night

The four sisters are asleep in their resting spot for the night. Vicky Jackson sleeps in the only second floor room above the garage. Sara whitewater sound asleep in one master bedroom of the house near the stairs leading to Vicky's room. Down the hall at the end the other two sisters resting with silence in their two bedrooms next to each other, Grace's is the other master bedroom while Courtney has a littlest room of the house yet has a bathroom that connects to Graces room while the main bathroom is in the middle of the house having a Jacuzzi bathtub and a shower. It's after midnight and all four scream loudly in their sleep waking themselves up in feeling marked scratched deeply in their pelvis area right above their vaginas'. Grace and Courtney go to their bathroom and Vicky quickly goes to the main bathroom as Sara meets her there. All four of them looking at what the hurt is above their vaginas'. "It hurts, what the hell?" Grace said, "Must got all of us, best to heal it, like a deep cut bit no need for stitches. There's cream in the cabinet," Courtney says looking at the cut. "What in the goodness," Sara said while she is holding her hand on the spot that burns with feeling cut. "You are too! Must be a mark, because it is looking like a cross yet upside down." Vicky mentions, "BURNS!" Sara said, "Yes it does hurt." Vicky agreed, then all four sisters hear a loud rattling in the house, they all met up in the living room to see about the noise. "Sounds like a rattle snake, y'all heard as well or you wouldn't move to see as we." Grace says looking around in the dark seeing only the moonlight beaming above through the windows from the northeast point with Courtney who followed her. "Yes, all got marks as well," Sara said to the other two sisters. "We need to do that protection spell, ASAP ladies!" Vicky excitedly says looking around to see if the serpent is appearing with the others. "Agreed! Everybody uses your knowledge and find a way, quickly." Grace says as she walks into the kitchen and turns on the lights. The other three sisters follow her,

Vicky gets a glass of water and takes her psych medicine, Sara goes to get her homemade tea with Trazadone effects, Courtney goes to seat herself at the table grabbing a pen and notepad from the counter.

Courtney writes down Holy Bible for her element of the protection spell. "Oh, I see, write down eagle beak and eagle feet for me," Vicky says as she seats herself next to Courtney having courage feeling going through her. Sara thinks while drinking her tea, having thoughts about the serpent being some kind of sickness or a mold in a soil and needs to be cleanse and mostly remove Its nature to life, "Write down pure soil and soil with mold for me." Sara said her elements for the spell. Grace standing next to Courtney, "A headache it's what this is. Put willow tree bark for me. Protection against hurt in the brain of our spell." Grace said as she is watching Courtney jot down the information.

Friday, March 17, 2017

"It still looks fresh, without the burning." Courtney says to Sara as they are getting ready to pray for their protection spell to be bound. "Yes, the mark will disappear, any doing it did will be entrap to not fold to the living." Sara explains to Courtney as Vicky and Grace are ready in the backyard of the evening to begin. Grace feels the breeze in the air having the last of the cold of the winter mixed with the new heat of the year. The northeast candles are lit first, and Sara continues to light the candles going clockwise direction till all twelve candles are lit. Fire is burning on the wick of all the white candles, Sara puts her element which is pure clean soil and soil with mold, "Cleanse!" Sara loudly said with might as the soils are put on the thick four-foot tree stump. "Protection!" Vicky said with might too putting Zoo kept eagle beak and eagle feet on the tree stump. "Mending!" Grace says with feeling the breeze like she just won a battle as she puts willow tree bark on the tree stump with the other elements. "Arch angel!" Courtney shouted with courageous emotion as she places an Holy Bible a hardcover on the tree stump to end the circle. "Bound us in healing with protection, Great Spirit!" Sara commanded with faith, "As the leader protects his flock being the alpha, do the same as we are your flock and you are the alpha, Great Spirit." Vicky says with mighty faith, "As the life of the green is able to heal the flesh, heal our whole existence, as animals protect the plants protect us in the wild nature of life," Grace firmly commands, "Believing the Christian said, will protect you against evil and heal you like a parent when come forth to you and obey your law, May we receive your love, Great Spirit!" Courtney prayed In consciousness of the nature about God ending the chant. Their hands tightly together in harmony while the fire on the candles blow out by no wind, Sight catching lightning strikes the tree stump with the objects then being on fire and then the candles begin to flame high lit fire in the silence with the breeze from the wind mixing in with the flames making it move in motions. The four sisters smile then they all feel a cooling sensation where they are marked above their vaginas in their pelvis region. They unfold their hands and touch the area with both hands under their colorful matching loose cotton pants. "It's gone!" Sara shouted. "Amen!" Courtney condones. "Yes, amen!" Grace agrees, being excited. "Yes, we are healed by faith and the elements of us connecting to the great spirit, Amen!" Vicky said being high in adrenaline. The objects on the tree stump are on fire still as they stare at it, "Lightening this time," Sara said looking at the fire upon the elements having no stress being lit. As all four stare with awe from knowingly the fire came from a lightning strike, in the dark of the beginning night forms a serpent from the darkness sight, he crawls without sight in the sisterhood's backyard looking upon them with only one thing in mind, to be free from their spell upon humanity that keeps them at bay about sinning in life, for the serpent job is to get man to sin and be astray from the father.

The Four women then take a step back and goes to their seats they have in the backyard right near the backdoor and on the patio. They sit and see the flames burning on the tree stump, "Wonder the flames might not stop burning for this one," Vicky said to her sisters, and they relax on their chairs. "Yes, lucky we are to come pass this book with the detail info for us to be witch and happen to have wisdom for us to be." Sara said opening her bottle filled with tea mixed with alike Trazadone psych medicine. The serpent then rattles his tail, "What! The rattle!" Grace shouted. All four cover their ears with their hands from the noise, the rattle goes on for fifteen minutes straight and the sisters are up around their backyard trying to find the cause of the noise which they know it's the serpent with two sisters not seeing it in flesh existence. Wet drops fall on the four sisters with every second the rain gets harder, making the fire unable to be aflame. "Let's go inside, it's been done anyways." Courtney suggested and the sisterhood goes in their paid off pure white colored house.

The Enemy & The Salvation

Friday, March 24 2017

"Very nice!" Vicky says in excitement seeing at least hundred and fifty birds to her naked eye flying around in her backyard having tall wooden fence around it's property mark. "Wealth, that's the symbol y'all doing its wealth," She mentions having a define of what the flock of birds are being. She walks further back towards the back fence passing two big trees that tangle with the neighbor's trees to the opening behind both trees that has sunshine everyday beaming in that spot beginning at noon which is the time now "Very well, the faithful." She says as she sees the birds following her and now flying above her. She looks on, the birds flight up to a higher height then aim down to her, flying to her falling lifeless once it's a close to her, "Ahh! Dead birds! All of them fell to me dead!" She hurries back in the house. "LADIES!", she screams for her sisterhood once in the kitchen from the backdoor. Sara walks in from the living room having nature sounds on the stereo system in there. Vicky grabs her, "Whoa! Easy on the shirt, very old had it since freshmen year." "Sorry! Come here, come to the backyard, tell the others." Vicky commanded as Grace walks in from being in her room, she mostly spends her time on the Internet searching for plants for sell, their seeds, roots, leaves, or the whole entire plant, also researching studies about plants and the entire medicine movement. "Backyard, why?" Grace asks as she follows Sara with Vicky leading the way. Courtney then walks in from being in her room seeing the backyard door open and walks out and sees her sisters in the back.

"Look!" Vicky shouts. "Tell me you see these dead birds, the dead robins." Sara speaks, "Yes, I see them, what happen!?" "We all can see them." Grace confirms as well. As Vicky starts to explain, Courtney shouts, "Move! Look behind you! Hurry!" Twelve huge stray tomcats jump the tall fence, "Oh moly!" Vicky screams as she runs towards the back door where Courtney is. Grace and Sara follows Vicky, all three make it to the back door, but the tomcats didn't followed them. "The birds are tasty to them, Vick." Sara says. "Birds!?" Courtney asks with confusion. "Tell her and tell us," Grace commanded watching the cats sniffing and clawing the birds to eat. "As I was out there, I see a lot of birds a flock or more than a flock flying around having a good time being them, I walk towards that spot where the sun shines directly, they followed me, I was taking it as a sign then suddenly they fly high up then fly toward me falling and becoming deceased." Vicky explains while shaking standing there as the brownish coated tomcats eat the birds. The three sisters then give Vicky a hug, "Keep the faith," Courtney says while done hugging her with the others. "We are strong, we are one," Sara says closing the backdoor as the tomcats' feast on all the birds. "Okay," Vicky sighs as she is getting a drink of Sara's tea with THC in it. Grace comes over Vicky, "Here take one, it's Trazadone pill same effects in one of our teas, it will calm you." Grace hands her the white powdered pill and Vicky takes it using the tea with THC to down it with. Sara goes to check if there is mail for its past twelve o clock. "So much for flight," Vicky sarcastically says standing next to Grace as Courtney is sitting at the kitchen table. "But deep in my existence there is faith for us to be strong, mostly me." Vicky adds. "There will be a good use one day for your ability to fly with a stick, just is not that popular need, but good to know." Courtney says in good spirit. "It's balance nature for the birds to give themselves to the cats," Grace mentions. Courtey sees a little stack of mail being thrown on the table by Sara. As Sara seats herself at the table Courtney goes through the mail. "All four of us got mail from the Social Security." She hands the mail to her sisters.

All four of them opens it and read, "Complete B.S.!" "What! No!" Sara and Courtney shouts at what they read, "First the birds the symbol of my connection and now our payments each month which is lasts for a lifetime are being discontinued, Damn man!" Vicky said in frustration still standing next to Grace. "Well, we have to wait to get our money back for we have to prove we cant survive without getting injected with medicine every month or regularly each year. I have money saved up from collecting all these years, I will buy a lawyer while calling social security to find out more, meanwhile hope y'all saved money for your-selves." Grace says having a solution. "Still doesn't clear the problem we have though, sis," Vicky said looking at her. "Even though our scar and the marking has cleared, it seems it hit us harder." Vicky continues now looking at Sara and Courtney and taking a drink of the influenced tea. "It blows my mind, we got to put all the stops before it hit us extremely harder." Sara says having her hands next to her forehead seating at the table while Courtney looks upon her and gets up from the table, walks over to the living room to turn on nature sounds to the loudest point where you can hear it through the house, and she goes back to the kitchen while the sounds of nature are in sound, she seats at the table. "Let's think, feed our head of thoughts of a defensive move," Grace then commands. All four sisters are in thought to end the effects and the life of the serpent before tragic hits them all four more with darkness that can't be overcome which they are feeling now after the events and the taking away of their financial wealth.

"It wants my connection to be dead and to be departed from the Great Spirit," Vicky says to her sisters, "What are we doing actually with our connection to the Great Spirit?" Vicky asks her sisters. "We are heal-ing the hurt bringing the light which is good to the darkness," Grace says, "Yeah but how? What made us know it this life?" Vicky asks again pointing out something. "The book called, Light Craft from there we learned as we went on." Sara answers Vicky. "So, we should summon the creator of the book, which is by Mary Norma, we summon her she can help us as being a tribe branched from her actual existence from using her book, matter of fact loving her book for it brought the supernatural to us, it made us who we are, and she will be able to destroy the serpent in our lives." Vicky explains while she is feeling the effects of the drink and not in shock anymore, not shaking, and not giving the slightest doubt while setting down her drink on the kitchen counter next to the refrigerator. Suddenly her tea drink mixed with THC begins boiling in the plastic cup and Vicky begins to puke all what she drank. She quickly gets a headache and her throat begins to sore while puking in the sink. "Ah... I feel sick." Vicky said with a sigh, "The cup! Quickly put it in the sink its melting!" Sara said to Grace, Grace who is standing next to Vicky and the cup being right near the kitchen sink as the melting plastic cup is on the counter connected to the sink, she quickly touches the cup and grabs it with one motion swings it to the sink with boiling hot tea pouring out of the cup, luckily Grace did not get burn with the quickness movement she did while holding the cup in slight grip. The cup is tilted in the sink having all the hot boiling tea pour down the drain.

"My throat is sore, and I have a slight headache," Vicky tells her sisters. Grace then goes to the bathroom, she looks in the bathroom sink cabinet, searches and finds a spray bottle like the ones found in stores for healing the sickness in the throat, yet more potent as she had made it herself six months ago. Grace walks in the kitchen holding the spray bottle and gives it to Vicky, "Here spray this every three hour, it should get healed." Grace said with determination it will work. Vicky grabs it and sprays her throat, "Cherry taste," Vicky mentions. "Yes, makes it has it effect with the taste," Grace explains. "We got to find a way to have all this stop," Vicky says with feeling her throat being slightly numb with a soothing feeling after spraying her throat with the homemade medicine. Then a quick pressure in her head made her close her eyes she sees a flash vision of a tombstone that read, "Vicky Jackson 1980-2018." "Whoa, I just had a vision of me dead!" Vicky says shockingly. Grace then touches her left shoulder, "What you saw, Hun?" "A tombstone that had my name on it and my death date year 2018. Vicky replies to Grace and Grace rubs her shoulder in comfort, "No one is going to die this time of our life, we will grow old together and live a wonderful positive energy from the Great Spirit," Grace says to her sister the one having experiencing the attack from the serpent firsthand as Grace and Sara have met the serpent seeing it with the naked eye. "Agreed, my sister. We will have our time with this enemy by glory of the Great Spirit, we will then defeat it," Courtney says in agreement with Grace giving hope to Vicky and the rest of her sisters.

"So, we summon the creator of our craft, the maker of the book we live by the excellence of this defensive move sit right to our image of sisterhood," Sara said wiping her short hair as relieving stress and breathes taking in what the type of attack the serpent been doing with realizing having the serpent appear, just appear to naked eye is the first form of its attack. "We get Mary Norma to appear, and it act will be a defensive attack by her appearing to us because we will shine the reason for her to come to us in the light so she will know," Sara continues while she gets up and goes to the refrigerator to pour her a glass of orange juice. "Simple attraction as a fruit will be our call to her," Sara said having a glass of orange juice for her to drink and she takes a drink. "Yes, our call will be her feast of energy to the living Great Spirit from the other side," Courtney adds seating still being more relaxed than her other sisters. "Okay, now how we, because I was thinking it's going to take our blood and our first ceremonial cup to attract light to her on the other side for the system of it came from her book." Vicky explains a way for them to do the summon spell that they think will help them to get the enemy to stop and be away from them in life continued. "Anything about giving life and light is the thought of our elements," Sara mentions her thoughts as she is looking at their first ceremonial cup that is on the kitchen round table and seats herself there with her glass of orange juice. "A crucifix for me meaning the way is Jesus Christ with the Great Spirit permitting him being the only way." Courtney said as she gets up to pour her a cold glass of tea mixed with the ingredients as an anti-anxiety medicine made from Grace. "Right the only way, well you need a tree to put the king on there, I will use roots of oak and maple tree for the life of it is useful as oxygen in the air or for man: carpentry, tree roots are mine." Grace said still standing next to Vicky looking upon her at times checking her wellness and seeing she is little weak for her throat needs attending to, but she seems okay to her as to do normal functions. Vicky looks upon Courtney going back to seat herself at the kitchen round table, "The slight headache was due to my sore throat for it gone now since the spray. Medicine is a symbol of health, as my choice is the symbol of heaven: the dove, it will flight with light to the other side for us to connect with Mary Norma as the crucifix is the gateway the trees give it breath." Vicky said explaining her side to the summon spell. "Rich, clean soil is mines, the place of the living God for man is here on earth, the other side of the other side." Sara says her input for the summon spell as she drinks her orange juice having almost finished the glass.

Grace hears water pouring and looks at the sink and sees a small stream of red color liquid pouring out of the faucet. "Hey, look! is that what I think it is," Vicky quickly sees the red color liquid pouring in the sink and the other two sisters gets out of their seats and go look at the sink with the other two staring. "What would it mean? Blood coming out of the kitchen sink." Vicky said with the other two now seeing it. "Quick get some in a cup," Sara commands her sisters. Vicky goes to the cabinet right beside her and grabs a cup then throws the cup to Grace as Grace catches it. The blood streams in the cup as Grace holds it under the faucet. "That's enough," Sara said as she grabs the cup from Grace and goes to the table sits the cup full of blood on there and seats herself as well. "What we do with the pouring blood that is coming out of the sink?" Vicky asks, "Pray and hopeful it will stop, I mean it all use is we can't get water right now." Courtney says as she seats herself at the table looking upon Sara staring at the blood in the glass. "Dear Great Spirit we are working to have you help us, guide us through the darkness and have the enemy be stop, amen." Grace quickly prayed and seats herself at the table. Vicky walks to the kitchen sink, turns on the water, and water comes overflowing the blood. She stares at the water thinking of her dead pet bird Jupiter being that calm noise to her as the water flowing. She turns off the water and sees no blood pouring out of the faucet now. "There!" She then walks to the round table and seats herself with her sisters.

"No blood no more?" Courtney asks Vicky, "Nope just run the water and it stopped," Vicky answers. Grace leans over the table to look at the blood in the cup next to Sara, "Its black, not even a reddish color in sight." Grace said as she seats herself back. "We will keep it in the cup and use this in our summon spell," Sara mentions. Courtney then grabs the cup and looks in it, "Yes, its black with a smell." Courtney then places the cup back next to Sara. "The next few days gather the needs and we should soon do this," Sara says looking at the black blood in the cup and sniffing it realizing it smells almost like a reptile blood for her uncle is in the reptile business, mostly selling the meat of alligators and she has smelt the blood of one before. "Also think of anything along the way if you can since like this blood here," Sara said.

Wednesday March 29, 2017

There are four 6ft candles for the four directions, eight 4ft candles for the pair of the corners making it twelve candles in a perfect circle in their backyard huge enough to fit at least ten people in the circle. The serpent who been existing in their backyard since the event of the birds, moves in the darkness of the beginning night in their backyard avoiding to be seen while it stayed in the dirt, and high up in the trees during the daytime while it motion itself to attack the sisterhood. "Beginning to light it all," Sara said motioning a lit match to the northeast point candles: the location where the sisterhood is spotted on the earth and she lights the candles going clock wise direction till all candles are lit from the northeast point. She then walks to the tree stump in the middle of the circle pours her rich clean soil process in a factory up northern state on the tree stump, "Come to the living of earth, defend our home." Sara commanded as the soil is on the tree stump and she stands. Vicky walks to the tree stump puts a carefully preserved dead white colored dove on the tree stump, "The bird shines the light of we which is good, may it guide you here to defend your kingdom," Vicky chants and stands eastside of the tree stump. Grace walks to the tree stump on the Southside of it and puts different kinds of tree roots with the other elements on the tree stump, "Breathe the light which is good of we to defend us in battle with its strength against the wicked," Grace commanded and stands. Courtney then walks to the tree stump on the Westside of it, puts the cup of blood that came from the kitchen sink, its blackness with an odor is an element and she places a crucifix on the tree stump as well, "The king is the way, forth your light against the darkness that threatens, sway to us by the king, sway away the enemy of our being." Courtney chants and stands. The four sisters in sisterhood hold each other hands around the tree stump, "We summon you Mary Norma!" the flame on the candles lit higher and brighter. At this time the serpent crawls near the circle from afar seeing the light from the candles, the backdoor to the end of the fence which is the back of the yard is 40 yards and the circle they made is closer to the back door. The serpents crawls and settles next to the southwest point of the outer circle near the candles but about 8 yards away is the sisterhood around the tree stump.

"We summon you Mary Norma in the Great Spirit, amen!" A fog suddenly comes in the circle like a cloud settled down on the ground. The sisterhood keep their hands held as they move their heads around to see each other and around to just see. Mary and Norma appears from the north east point of the circle through the thick fog walking standing next to Sara and Vicky. "Sisters!" Mary loudly mentions their sight to the sisterhood. "Two?" Vicky said, "Whoa!" Grace excitedly said. "Yes, twins, I'm Norma and this is Mary the ones youse are connecting to," Norma explains. "You guys are extremely beautiful like your skin is glowing," Sara mentions. "Yes it's the light of father and our light is good with father, the same light in our existence is the light that's going to help you in need," Norma also explains. "Drink the water in that cup," Mary commanded. "Water?" Courtney asks shockingly. "The cup with the blood in it," Grace answers her. Courtney then grabs the cup off the tree stump and sees pure water inside the dark colored cup. "Look it's water," Courtney says as she passes it to Sara. Sara then looks in the cup, "Yes, the black blood is gone," Sara said. "Yes, each of you drink it and the enemy shall not be with you anymore," Norma says holding hands with her twin sister. The serpent hears this and crawls from the southwest end to make itself known to the sisterhood, "How dare youse! Excuse my anger, I'm the mightiest beast in the garden of life!" the serpent said having being rise three foot higher than the sisterhood right near them. "Hurry drink! Each take a swallow!" Mary commands. Sara then drinks a swallow, gives the cup to Vicky, Vicky takes a swallow of the pure water, she gives the cup to Grace, Grace quickly takes a swallow , and she gives the cup to Courtney. Courtney stares at her sisters for a moment taking what's going on in, "Dare me to destroy youse for good!" the serpent loudly said with a hiss, Courtney then quickly drinks a swallow of the water as she sets the cup down in the tree stump the serpent raises his tail swaying it fast towards the sisterhood around the tree stump, "Ahh!" all four screams, the tail comes an inch close to the sisterhood in full force suddenly the serpent dissolves in water bleeding through the grassy soil.

"Holy water, it's what youse drank, it conquers the wicked and strengthens the light which is good," Norma explains. "Use the water wisely, when there is a need, and make it last. The spell the enemy was attacking you for gives us joy in the tender light of life with father," Mary says. "Always keep faith in father, and obey the natural laws," Norma commands the sisterhood. Norma and Mary starting going in a circle holding hands, giggling and morphing to a child from appearing to be adults, "Ring around the Rosie, the serpent being nosey, pray to the king, holiness lights out being, Ring around a Rosie, the serpent now knows we, light from the king, disappears the enemy from our being," the twin sisters sings dissolving into thin air, the fire lit candles blows out and the sisterhood stands with joy staring at each other then the fire aflame high on each candle lighting the area in a circle in their backyard as the moon light shines brighter in the region.

"The candles are well lit, and that just happen guys. Keep the faith and obey the great spirit. Our white light craft will ever be strong in it's energy to be alive by our existence," Sara said unfolding her hands from her sisters grip. "We got natural Holy water, dip small amount into another glass of water and boom! More Holy water," Vicky says as she departs her grip from holding hands too. Sara leaves then Vicky, Grace and then Courtney walking towards the backdoor. They stand at the doorway and look at the burning candles being lit aflame brightly in their backyard, and they are having harden faith in what they are, witches for the Great Spirit.

www.ingramcontent.com/pod-product-compliance
Lightning Source LLC
Chambersburg PA
CBHW061408160726
47995CB00002B/518